Bear in Sunshine
Oso bajo el Sol

Stella Blackstone
Debbie Harter

Barefoot Books
step inside a story

**Bear likes to play
when the sun shines.**

A Oso le gusta jugar cuando el sol brilla.

Bear likes to sing
when it rains.

A Oso le gusta cantar
cuando llueve.

**He flies his red kite
when it's windy.**

Él vuela su cometa roja
cuando hace viento.

**When it's icy,
he skates in the lane.**

Cuando hay hielo, él patina en el camino.

**Bear likes to paint
when it's foggy.**

A Oso le gusta pintar
cuando hay neblina.

When it's stormy,
he hides in his bed.

Cuando hay tormenta, se esconde en su cama.

When it snows, he likes to make snow-bears.

Cuando nieva, le gusta hacer osos de nieve.

When the moon shines,
he stands on his head.

Cuando la luna brilla,
él se para de cabeza.

Whatever the weather, snow, rain, or sun,

Como esté el tiempo,
con nieve, lluvia o sol,

**Bear always knows
how to have fun!**

¡Oso siempre sabe cómo divertirse!

Spring
la primavera

Summer
el verano

Autumn
el otoño

Winter
el invierno

Vocabulary / Vocabulario

weather – el tiempo

sun – el sol

moon – la luna

rain – la lluvia

kite – la cometa

wind – el viento

ice – el hielo

fog – la neblina

storm – la tormenta

snow – la nieve

Barefoot Books
2067 Massachusetts Ave
Cambridge, MA 02140

Barefoot Books
29/30 Fitzroy Square
London, W1T 6LQ

First published in the United States of America by Barefoot Books,
Inc and in Great Britain by Barefoot Books, Ltd in 2001
This bilingual Spanish edition first published in 2017

Translated by Leticia Meza-Riedewald
Reproduction by Grafiscan, Verona, Italy
Printed in China on 100% acid-free paper
This book was typeset in Futura and Slappy
The illustrations were prepared in watercolor,
pen and ink, and crayon

ISBN 978-1-84686-389-9

British Cataloguing-in-Publication Data: a catalogue record
for this book is available from the British Library

Library of Congress Cataloging-in-Publication Data
is available under LCCN 2009003087

13 15 17 19 18 16 14 12